FIVE WEE PŪTEKETEKE

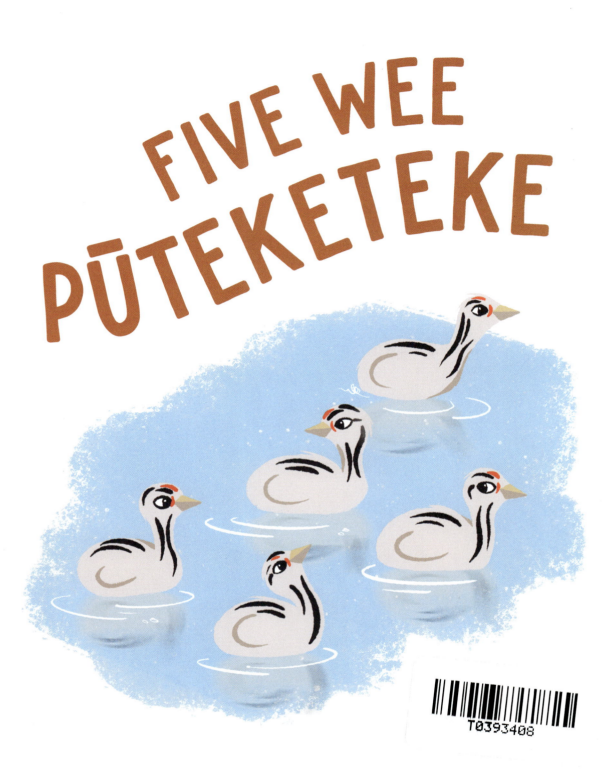

Nicola Toki
& Jo Pearson

Five wee pūteketeke went swimming one day over the roto and far away.

Pūteketeke parents carry their babies on their backs.

. . . and only whā iti pūteketeke came back.

They make nests that float on the water, sometimes attached to reeds.

Four wee pūteketeke went swimming one day,
learning to duck and dive their way.

. . . and only toru iti pūteketeke came back.

Three wee pūteketeke went swimming one day, finding new fun ways to play.

Stoats and ferrets can attack pūteketeke.

. . . and only rua iti pūteketeke came back.

Two wee pūteketeke went swimming one day,
their pāpā got them food before they went away.

The parents vomit up fish and feathers to feed their chicks.

One of them said,
"I don't like this snack!" . . .

. . . and only tahi iti pūteketeke came back.

They do this dance, called the 'ghostly penguin', to show off.

One wee pūteketeke went swimming one day,
watching her parents rise and sway.

The little one said,
"I'll give that a crack!" . . .

. . . and no wee pūteketeke came back.

The māmā and pāpā both sit on the nest and look after the babies together.

Māmā pūteketeke went swimming one day, to find a safe place for her babies to stay.

Someone built nests for the Pūteketeke on Lake Wānaka and the birds started breeding on them straight away!

She found a big floating nest on a wooden raft and ALL FIVE wee pūteketeke came home at last!

PŪTEKETEKE – WHAT'S ALL THE FUSS ABOUT?

The pūteketeke, also known as the Australasian crested grebe, was a little-known bird until 2023 when Forest & Bird held a 'Bird of the Century' competition to celebrate its 100th birthday. Many people wanted iconic birds such as the kiwi or kākāpō to win this honour, and there were even some extinct birds, such as the huia, that were in the running.

A famous American-British TV host, John Oliver, learned about the competition and decided he wanted the pūteketeke to win. He loved them. He called them 'weird puking birds' and built enormous puppets to celebrate them. He helped inspire 300,000 people in almost 200 countries around the world to vote for his favourite bird!

Despite the 'American interference' in the voting, the pūteketeke is actually an amazing species which needs a lot more attention, so it is a worthy winner!

In the 1980s there were probably only 200 of them left in Aotearoa. Pūteketeke are found in high country lakes across the South Island, and they are in trouble, due to predators such as stoats, which take their chicks.

Pūteketeke are easily disturbed by boats, cars and predators on the lake shore where they like to build their floating nests. In 2012 there was only one breeding pair of pūteketeke left in Lake Wānaka. Then a man called John Darby built a nesting platform for them to safely lay their eggs and raise their chicks. The pūteketeke moved onto the nest platform straight away! Since then, there have been over 450 chicks raised on the nesting platforms in Lake Wānaka.

First published in 2024

Text © Nicola Toki
Illustrations © Jo Pearson

All rights reserved. No part of this book may be reproduced or transmitted in any form or by any means, electronic or mechanical, including photocopying, recording or by any information storage and retrieval system, without prior permission in writing from the publisher.

Allen & Unwin
Level 2, 10 College Hill, Freemans Bay
Auckland 1011, New Zealand
Phone: (64 9) 377 3800
Email: auckland@allenandunwin.com
Web: www.allenandunwin.co.nz

83 Alexander Street
Crows Nest NSW 2065, Australia
Phone: (61 2) 8425 0100

A catalogue record for this book is available from the National Library of New Zealand.

ISBN 978 1 99100 689 9
Design by Kate Barraclough
Set in Adobe Garamond Pro and Crayon En Folie
Printed and bound in China by 1010 Printing Ltd

10 9 8 7 6 5 4 3 2 1